The River

ENCOUNTERS WITH WAR

Cheddar 2020: celebrating the seventy-fifth
anniversary
of VE Day

Published in 2020 by Roundhouse Books

Printed by Kindle Direct Publishing

Text: authors as listed in contents. The copyright for each
story or article rests with the author thereof.
All rights reserved.

ISBN: 9798613056705

Contributors

Margaret Castle

Jennie Colton

Angela Cornborough

Phyllis Goddard

Sally Green

Penny Harden

Dianne Long

Jude Painter

Sue Purkiss (Editor)

Heather Redman

Caroline Woolley

Introduction

The Riverside Writers is a group of writers which meets once a week in Cheddar. We have produced two previous anthologies – *Through the Barn Door* and *Just Write* – and when we heard that Chaff (the Cheddar Arts Fringe Festival) was this year taking as its theme the seventy-fifth anniversary of VE Day, we decided to join in with a new collection of stories and articles. All the proceeds will go to the Cheddar Youth Trust, a charity which provides grants to young people. It seems fitting that we should be looking forwards as well as back.

Three of the group could actually remember the war. The rest of us had to rely on stories told by others – often by parents – and on research. The pieces are not all specifically about VE Day itself: it became very apparent as we discussed our ideas that much as VE Day deserved to be celebrated, it was not in truth the end of the war for those who had lived through it. The lives of the evacuees, of the men and women who were in the forces, of those who were taken prisoner and of those who stayed at home, were all changed during those years – not necessarily in obvious ways. These stories, memoirs and articles reflect that.

They are in alphabetical order according to the

authors' names, and there is a brief introduction before each piece explaining its context. If there are any mistakes or omissions, blame the editor!

We hope you enjoy the book.

Sue Purkiss (Editor)

Memories of war
By Margaret Castle

As a child during the war, Margaret lived in Southampton with her mother. Her father was away for almost the duration, first fighting, and then in prison camps – so when he came home, he was a stranger to her... (Ed)

Earliest memories

My first memory is of a night when my mother got somebody – it may have been my grandfather, who had a petrol allowance because of Home Guard duties – to drive us over to my Great Aunt Ethel's house on the other side of the New Forest from Southampton where we lived. The docks were on fire again; this time it was around 1942. I was told not to look. I could only have been two plus, but I recall peeping out from under a rug to get a glimpse, and I saw the whole world on fire to our left where the docks were.

Another time, back at home, we became accustomed to the drone of enemy planes on their way to bomb the Spitfire factory and other important sites. There was no danger to us on their way in, so, in spite of the warning siren, when we were supposed to go into our Morrison shelter in the dining room, it was tempting to watch planes overhead.

One day I was called outside to have a good look and was informed that the sign on the side was a swastika.

The Morrison shelter I mentioned was made of iron, top and bottom, with iron uprights at its corners. Its sides were re-enforced open grid, like square trellis. We were supposed to sleep inside, but my mother hauled a mattress from the bedroom and slung it on top. Measurements: 2metres long, 1.2 metres wide and 75cm high. If the siren went, we grabbed blankets and clambered in underneath, closing the grid behind. Miss Jenkins from next-door-but-one joined us sometimes. She had a very long plait which at night she allowed to hang down her back, but she made earphones of it for daytime appearances. On some occasions when we'd had a warning and the three of us were tucked inside, if there hadn't been an all-clear for hours, my mother would crawl out to fetch the primus; a pan with some dripping and some bread. She would then make the three of us fried bread.

Fortunately, we didn't catch fire, or get burnt or bombed out. Others, of course, did.

Lemonade for pre-embarkation troops, Southampton, 1944

It was warm and sunny that day. My mother was busy. A big day, I could tell, but why, I didn't know yet. It was 1944, late spring. I was almost four and a half. That morning I was given an unusual chore.

"Go across the road and ask at the shop for as many of their lemonade crystals as they'll let you have," said Mother.

I was given money in a purse. I don't remember if coupons were involved, but off I scampered to the bottom of our turning, called Pine Drive, which was in fact a gravel crescent with bungalows and houses scattered around its edges. We lived in the country above Southampton, surrounded by woods. The woods were critical, I was to discover.

On my return with the bag of crystals, I was sent around the turning to our neighbours to borrow beakers. Back at home, the card table had been set up outside our gates, a cloth covering it. I was told to line up as many beakers as I could at the front. Then we both mixed the crystals with water in a variety of jugs, until the crystals dissolved. I fetched the milk covers to protect the lemonade from flies. These covers were nets with beads sewn on to weigh them down. Once the jugs had been placed at the back of the table, I had to stand by the table and wait with my mother.

Suddenly there was the sound of heavy boots on the gravel as soldiers marched along Pine Drive to pass before us. We had already set out some beakers of lemonade in readiness. They must have been in relaxed marching mode as they paused, took a swig, exchanged some cheery comment, nodded a thanks and marched on towards the woods at the top of the Drive. There seemed to be hundreds of them. There was no chance to wash up, so the beakers were re-used again and again. I think everyone got a drink.

This was a personal contribution to our soldiers setting up their pre-embarkation camp inside the woods, totally disguised from the air. We discovered later that they were preparing for D-Day, the Normandy Landings. My gang of friends played around between the tents, chasing each other along duckboards. Then, just as suddenly as they'd come, one night the soldiers had gone. Our black Scottie dog disappeared too, the back gate left swinging open. I was informed the soldiers had probably taken him, hoping to smuggle him on board as a mascot. I couldn't understand how anyone would think they could take a dog to war. But we never saw him again. My mother thought he'd have been discovered and removed, pre-boarding.

I don't remember grieving very much, possibly because, suddenly, the Americans arrived. On searching the internet, it appears that they were more probably Canadian, but we knew them as American. We repeated the lemonade welcome. Here the similarity ended. The first thing I noticed was that these men were very smartly dressed. They had pressed trousers, creases down the front. Our soldiers wore coarse fabric uniforms and looked tired. I realize now that they'd probably already been fighting and were about to go back. The Americans were fresh, good-humoured and friendly to us children; generous with sweets and money. They didn't enjoy camping in the woods, however, where most of them showered outside with a strange pulley water system behind sacking and corrugated iron. Toilets were dug out of the ground.

Some officers requested the use of bathrooms for a soak in return for food, which was forbidden but very common. I clearly remember answering the front door to a uniformed man who carried a rolled-up towel under one arm. Following earlier instructions, I pointed to the bathroom door, which was straight ahead. He smiled, nodded and walked briskly to the bathroom.

One day I found a shiny bucket by our back gate with a large joint of meat poking out. I rushed indoors to report my find and was instructed not to talk about it. It was hidden in the loft against any inspection. Two people did come and question my mother and other families in the turning: Ministry of Food perhaps? I remember any extra food was shared out amongst the neighbours.

During the Americans' stay, they must have had quite a bit of spare time. They requested permission to give all the children in our turning a ride. We were going all the way to

Southampton Pier in DUKWs, six wheeled amphibious vehicles. These hefty vehicles, without any concession to the gradient, drove straight down the slipway, next to the pier and into deep water, spray flying everywhere and children screaming as they took us around Southampton Water in these unusual vehicles.

These soldiers were inclined to leave random brown paper bags in bushes, with hard biscuits and harder chocolate. None of it was nice and we weren't that hungry. Years later I asked my mother what she thought and she guessed it was surplus survival rations, which they thought we needy British might find useful. We never discovered why they hid them in the hedges and bushes.

When they finally left in broad daylight, unlike our soldiers, who had disappeared in the night, they waved as we ran behind their vehicles, scattering change for us.

A year later: VE Day 8th May 1945

Everyone got the bus into Southampton - I had been informed that it was an historic day and so we should be there. I was perched up on the wall of the white Civic Centre building, in the middle of town, where, when we were being bombed on 6th November in 1940 in daylight, my Auntie Vera had lain injured in the bombed-out section for two days. It had been a direct hit. A 500lb bomb killed thirty five people: fourteen were children having an art class in the basement. They eventually found Auntie Vera trapped under debris in the Library. She recovered but became asthmatic.

Also around that time, my paternal grandparents' road was almost entirely flattened. Amazingly, but typical of the randomness of bombing, they were unhurt, but the Carter family next door, my grandparents' friends, were all killed. Doing a little research I have discovered that Hermann Goering, head of the Luftwaffe remarked, on viewing an aerial shot of our Civic Centre, that it appeared like a piece of cake and that he was going to 'cut himself a slice.'

So there I was on the wall of the Civic Centre, on 8th of May, considerably bewildered by the idea of Victory in Europe. What did it mean? There were hordes of people singing and waving flags. But as far as we knew, my father was still a prisoner of war in Stalag 383, Bavaria. What we didn't know was that the Germans had abandoned the camp around 22nd April 1945. Years later, my father would explain – briefly – that they were left to survive as best they could. The Germans had almost no food themselves. The situation was chaotic and still dangerous. There was no-one to organise a rescue. Malnutrition was rife. He and two fellow Royal Engineer friends left the camp together. It rained and they got soaked but they found a barn where they took off their uniforms, stuffed them with straw to try to dry them out, and spent the night taking it in turns to be the one in the middle, to try to keep themselves warm. The next day, they moved on. A German saw them in the street. They were lucky as he was friendly and gave them half a loaf of black bread, when he probably had very little himself. They wandered about for two or three days.

Eventually, some Americans in a jeep came across them and picked them up. There was considerable confusion everywhere; thousands of men waiting for transport. They were eventually flown home: in my father's case, in the bomb bay of a Lancaster, along with many other men. We received a telegram, undated, which I've still got, just confirming he'd arrived. Even then there were de-briefings before he was allowed to come home.

VE Day was over and my father was home, but the effects of all he had gone through were long-lasting and affected all of us. The war had a very long reach, and didn't just affect those who fought in it.

Margaret as a child

Wartime Wedding
By Jennie Colton

This piece is based very closely on Jennie's mum's memories of her wartime wedding. (Ed)

As she watched her beautiful grand-daughter walking serenely up the aisle in her stunning designer wedding dress, with her three lovely bridesmaids dressed in matching turquoise silk dresses, Edith was reminded of her own wedding day all those years ago. It had been December 26th 1942, when World War Two was in its third, terrible year. At twenty-one she had been a young bride by today's standards, but the war seemed to make everyone grow up more quickly. The food shortages, the bombing raids and the sense of an unknown future all had an effect on people's mentality and outlook.

A picture of Ron as a handsome eager young man came flashing into her mind. They had been married for fifty two years but sadly, he had died in his seventies, leaving her a widow for a long time now. His work as a builder and then as a supervisor in a munitions factory had spared him from conscription and after a lengthy courtship, they had finally named the day. She remembered the sacrifices her parents, brother, sister, aunts, uncles and cousins had all made, saving coupons so she could not only have a dress from a shop but two bridesmaids' dresses, food for the reception and even a wedding cake. The wedding cake had been the present from her soon-to-be mother-in- law, who had saved all her sugar rations for several months to make sure there was enough sugar to ice the cake.

Unlike the beautiful expensive dress her grand-daughter was wearing, her dress had been simple, with a demure high neck and tiny buttons from neck to waist. It had been made from parachute silk and the bridesmaids' dresses, although the same design, had been different colours. Her bouquet had been just a bunch of late blooming chrysanthemums from a neighbour's greenhouse.

She was brought back from her reverie by the vicar's words, spoken loudly and very clearly,

"I now pronounce you man and wife!"

As the happy smiling couple went into the vestry with their witnesses to sign the register, Edith thought to herself how strange life was: it could all have been so different. She almost hadn't got married on that day and if she hadn't, then today could not have happened.

The problem had been the taxi that was supposed to be taking her and the bridesmaids to the church, about three-quarters of a mile away. The taxi belonged to a work colleague who ran a small taxi service as a side-line – not very easy with petrol-rationing. The time to leave came and went with no sign of the taxi and Edith became more and more upset, but was absolutely adamant that she would not walk the long road to the church in the bitter December cold in her thin wedding dress. If the taxi didn't come, she would not get married.

Fortunately, the driver did arrive, albeit thirty minutes late – he had been unable to start the car in the cold and had flooded his engine after too many attempts to get it going. After that, everything went well. The reception in the village hall – and particularly the wedding cake – were much enjoyed; in those times of austerity, any extra luxuries were very much appreciated.

She smiled to herself, as she thought about her honeymoon night. No honeymoon at all, just a small bedroom in her parents-in-law's house, where the walls were thin and there never seemed to be much privacy. Unlike, her granddaughter and husband, who would be jetting off to the Maldives for a romantic, sunny holiday the next day. How different it all was now.

As the organist enthusiastically struck up the first chords of the Wedding March, her granddaughter and new husband walked down the aisle, smiles radiating from their faces. A large tear rolled down Edith's face.

"Silly old woman," she thought to herself. "Oh, but I do love a good wedding!"

Jennie's parents' wedding

The Station
By Angela Cornborough

Angela writes: 'My father was in a reserved occupation as a railway engineer when war broke out, and it was not until late 1941/early 1942 that he was eventually called up. He joined the Royal Navy and spent much of his time on convoy duty in the Atlantic. He said he was always confident that he would survive the war, though he often felt guilty that he had when so many of his friends had not. He rarely spoke in detail about his experiences and when he did, his stories always had a humorous slant. The following fictional account is loosely based on true events that occurred in Bristol.'

War makes heroes or cowards of us all. I have myself down as the latter, though in fairness I haven't truly been put to the test yet.

I volunteered as soon as war was declared – not that I wanted to fight, I just thought it was my duty – but because I was an engineer on the railways they wouldn't take me - 'reserved occupation' you see. So, I carried on working as if nothing had changed.

Things *are* different obviously. Resources are getting more and more limited and trying to keep everything running is taxing all of us. We are often the target in bombing raids because they know the railways are the country's lifeline. Last night a rogue bomber, who'd either missed his target or found himself with a spare bomb, decided the goods yard would be a good place to drop it. It was cloudy and no one was expecting a raid. The sirens hadn't sounded and he just appeared out of nowhere in a break in the cloud. He didn't hit any of the locomotives, thank goodness, but it took us all day to make good the mess he'd made of the lines and get the trains running again

The timetable has gone by the board anyway; trains come and go when they can and we are constantly patrolling the line. I have joined the Local Defence Volunteers – the Home Guard they call it now – and I often find myself on a lonely stretch of line on the lookout for saboteurs or spies.

'Who goes there? Friend or foe?' is the challenge if anything so much as moves. What spy worth his salt would answer *foe,* I laugh? And, more to the point, what would I do if he did?

It's been a long old day. But I'm off now, home for a bath and some supper… Except that Gerry has other ideas; there's the bloody siren again and there's a troop train just about to enter the section. They'll divert it into one of the far-off sidings I hope, though there's not much cover.

My God! There's dozens of the bastards – I don't think I've ever seen that many planes in one go. And I've never known them come while it's still light. Looks like it'll be a long old night too.

It's the noise that gets me – that whistle as the bomb

drops and the wait to see where it hits. The first one crashes into the end of the station building. I dive to the floor with my hands over my head. The blast is ear-shattering and as I try to get up, I feel disorientated and unsure what to do. ARP wardens blowing whistles are trying to martial people off the platforms and into the tunnels. They don't need me so I run towards the locomotives in the sidings. I wave my arms and scream at the troops: 'Get off the train, get off the train,' but I doubt they can hear me. The driver and fireman have climbed down from the locomotive and are running along opening doors so the men can get out.

Fires are breaking out everywhere and as I run to cross the lines, one of the planes lets rip a volley of bullets that ping and ricochet off the rails. I dive for the floor again, reluctant to move now for fear his friends will see this as good sport. I'm a sitting duck though, so I get up and streak across the lines – my PT teacher from school would be proud of me. I almost reach the far side when another plane strafes the platform. This time I keep going. And then all hell breaks loose.

Bombs are falling all around me and the troop train has taken a direct hit. The engine explodes; flames, ash and steam shoot up into the air. It fizzes and spits until the boiler is empty and finally dies. The blast knocks me off my feet and I can only crawl along the ground.

Alongside is the yard and the stables and I can see smoke billowing from the open doorway. Horses are whinnying in terror and their hooves ring as they rear up and clang back down onto the cobbled floor. They beat at the wooden doors trying to escape. But I'm more concerned for the troops on that train.

I seem to have acquired a bucket of sand – I don't remember how – though what use it will be I can't imagine. As I run towards the train someone shouts:

'Get those bloody horses out.' He isn't shouting at me, he can't be; I'm terrified of horses. But when I look, he's pointing at me, calling my name.

'Bill, Bill, get the horses out!' No! I look at the stables, properly ablaze now, then at the train, then at the warden – one of the station staff obviously. I can't see who it is but he evidently knows me. I hesitate and he shouts again.

'For God's sake Bill; the horses!'

I run at the stables, still carrying the bucket of sand, which I hope might prove useful at last. I plunge into the smoke and flames, scattering the sand behind me to smother some of the smaller fires. And then I stop dead in my tracks. The biggest horse I have ever seen in my life, rearing, towering over me, snorting, thrashing, whinnying. I can't! I can't! I don't know which one of us is the most frightened. I climb over the wooden gate, afraid to open it for fear he'll bolt or trample me. I try to stay calm and speak soothingly.

'Whoa boy, steady!' But he knows I'm more scared than he is and he wants to kill me. I'm very conscious of the crashing hooves as he rears time and again.

'Throw something over his eyes,' shouts a voice. I grab a blanket and lob it over his head. Instantly he stops rearing, though he's trembling all over. The owner of the voice thrusts a halter into my hand as he runs past me with a horse in tow and somehow, I get it over my horse's head, though he thrashes and almost rips my arm out of its socket. I open the gate and make to lead him out but now he won't budge. I curse at the stupid so-and-so as he treads on my foot.

'Hold him on a short rein and slap his read end,' comes the voice again. Easier said than done, for his rear end is a long way from his front and in very close proximity to those deadly hooves. But I manage a hefty whack and he lurches forward and we are off at a run. He has managed to toss the blanket aside but he can smell freedom and is happy to follow where I lead.

We burst out into the yard but the scene that greets us is like an artist's impression of hell. Everywhere is on fire; people are shouting, screaming, running, calling for stretchers. A barrage balloon has been hit and has dropped onto some trees and they too are now ablaze. And the smell – I realise it's burning flesh from the troops who didn't get off the train in time.

My eyes are streaming and I'm not sure whether it's from the smoke in the stables or whether I'm crying. It doesn't matter I suppose. I retch and vomit.

The horse brings me back to myself. He pulls on the rein, still terrified, as being out in the open doesn't bring either of us any comfort. I'm not sure what to do with him but then a stable boy runs up and relieves me of my burden. My arms ache, my eyes sting, I am coughing and spluttering but I know I have to go back in and do it all again.

The bombers are long gone and the all clear has sounded but the fires still rage. Everywhere is chaos. We only lost one of the horses, though I feel bad about that; I should have reacted quicker. I can see from the line of bodies that the troops on the train did not fare so well.

Relieved of my equine responsibilities I am drafted in for stretcher duties. The stretchers are made of wire mesh and I keep thinking it must hurt when I see it cutting into men's faces where they have been lain on their sides. I know they're dead but it still upsets me.

It's gone midnight and the worst seems to be over. A few small fires burn here and there but these can be beaten out easily. I slide down a wall and sit on my haunches. It all seems surreal. 'It'll all be over by Christmas,' they said – ha! what a laugh. I wonder how long it *will* last and what good will come of it. They didn't achieve much the first time round.

I try to hate the enemy, but I can't. There's probably some poor sod over there doing and feeling exactly the same as me. Every man that dies is somebody's father, husband, son. They must be suffering the same as we are.

I drop my head on my chest and – hero or coward – give thanks that I'm alive.

Angela's father

The Housing Ladder
By Phyllis Goddard

Phyllis was a hugely valued member of the group for several years. Well into her nineties now, she is no longer able to join us, but she was happy for this piece to be included in the book – it first appeared in an earlier collection. Phyllis was a young woman living in London during the war: in another piece from the earlier book, she recalled walking home during the Blitz. She remembers looking down at the Thames, and says quietly, "It was like a river of blood." (Ed)

In May 1945 my husband and I returned to civilian life after our time in the forces. After VE Day it should have been a joyous time, but there was a problem facing us and so many other people whose homes had been lost in the bombing: we had nowhere to live.

My husband's mother had been forced out of her house because it had been made unsafe by bomb blast, and she had been moved to a London County Council house in Morden, Surrey. My own home had been completely demolished and my parents and sister were living in a Nissen hut in Dulwich. Because of these arrangements, it appeared no-one else in the families was entitled to be housed.

My husband was far from well; he had served in Malta

for two years and then moved to the tiny island of Leros, where after a three day battle he and the few remaining members of his regiment were taken prisoner by the invading Germans and, in the middle of winter, transported to Leipzig in northern Germany.

One would have thought that we had enough 'points' to entitle us to some accommodation, but apparently not. My mother in law was kind enough to give us a room in her house. It was small, but we did have a roof over our heads. When the baby came and her own daughter and husband moved into another room, life was far from harmonious. The day had to come and it did: my mother-in-law and I had a stormy argument and I walked out, just remembering to push some essentials into a bag for the baby. I did leave a note for my husband to read, when he came home from work, telling him I would be with my mother. That night I sat in an armchair, the baby slept in his pram and my husband went back to his mother's house. There was nothing else to do for the moment.

That night I had plenty of time to think. We had tried every avenue possible to find somewhere to live and now I decided we had to do something drastic, but what? Then I remembered the great big building on London Bridge, which housed the London County Council's offices. I would go tomorrow and plead my case. It was the only hope left to us.

No use writing letters, we had done that and they had been no help at all.

At ten am the next morning I arrived at the door of the housing department's offices at County Hall. I was ready with my request. I had rehearsed it over and over again. I sat on one of the chairs in the long corridor nursing the sleeping baby and waiting my turn in a short queue. The preliminary conversation went quite well, but when I had answered all the clerk's questions there was a rather long silence. The baby began to cry and to quiet him I got up and walked up and down by the desk. The clerk moved to another area and my heart began to beat fast. The baby stopped crying and the clerk came back.

"If you will fill in this form we will do all we can to help you. We will contact you by post".

"You can't contact me by post, I have no address," I said quietly. "That's why I'm here. I'll wait in the corridor."

Wait in the corridor I did, except for trips to the toilet to feed the baby and change his nappies. I ate my sandwich and drank water from the drinking fountain and I waited. The staff came and went, making the odd remark. I expect they thought I was mad. There was a lot going on, I wasn't bored, but I began to get anxious when the clock showed it was 4pm. The offices would close in about an hour – what then? I eventually heard my name being called and I went into the office, hoping there was some good news.

Instead, when I sat down at the desk , the clerk picked up a sheet of paper and said, "If you can find somewhere to go tonight, we have found you a place in a Rest Centre at Clapham. It's pretty grim but it will get you on to the housing ladder. They will provide you and your husband with beds, meals and laundry facilities and you can use the accommodation twenty four hours a day." Nothing left there to my imagination, but it sounded like heaven to me.

I met my husband at the station as we had arranged. He agreed it was better than nothing, but I knew he was unhappy that we had come to such a pass. Little did we realise we still had a long way to go before we could say we had a 'home', but it was better than nothing and we would be together.

The Rest Centre was a convent, large and imposing, requisitioned for the use of the homeless. We were shown our accommodation, a large room sectioned off in into four cubicles by canvas walls, each one housing people on the housing waiting list. Two camp beds and a chest were all there was in each one, but we could get our pram in and the baby slept quite happily there. The meals provided were plain, but well-cooked and ample and there were facilities for washing and drying and a separate room for ironing.

The sleeping conditions though needed sorting out or we would be walking about like zombies. The couple in the next cubicle smoked and the baby cried most of the night. The only window in the room was in a cubicle and was never opened, so the atmosphere by the morning was unbearable. We went to the office and explained and the warden agreed that it was far from satisfactory, but there were no vacant cubicles. However there was the 'ironing room', and there was room there for us and the pram, but only if we agreed to use the room for sleeping between nine at night and eight in the morning. There was also an empty cupboard that we could use. Our luck was in for once.

We lived like this for several weeks. My husband went off to work each morning from the station across the road and I walked most days to my parents' Nissen hut in West Dulwich. The other homeless people in the centre were very friendly and we all shared the joy of those whose names appeared on the notice board when there was accommodation available and they were top of the waiting list.

Then our turn came and a letter arrived, with an appointment to view an LCC maisonette in Carshalton. I had, by now, made peace with my mother-in-law and she and I went together to the viewing. My husband had gone off that morning to sit an insurance exam. As we parted he said,

"As long as it has four safe walls, a door and a key, sign anything." Which of course I did!

We moved into the maisonette with only a bed, a cot,

two orange boxes, two old kitchen chairs and enough cutlery and saucepans for two people. Furniture and curtains had to wait until we received the government coupons .

As the years went by we moved twice into larger houses until we had saved enough money to build our own house. We needed a licence to buy a plot of land and just couldn't get one, the reason being that we already had a house. I went into action again. This time by letter, explaining that we lived in a council house and by building our own house we would be making ours available for someone else. Back came a reply to the effect that the waiting list was so long that one place made no difference. It just made so much more work.

We did eventually get a license and were able to step up one more rung of the housing ladder by having our own house built, and we spent the next thirty odd years bringing up our family in a lovely spot in Bexley, Kent. We lived a full, interesting life there, full of joys and sorrows and supported by so many friends and neighbours, but in the end we agreed that the time had come to move, hopefully for the last time, and to Cheddar, where we eventually found the bungalow we had been looking for. No licenses or waiting lists! This time, in just a few weeks, we had sold our Bexley house and were settling into Churchside, so named because it backed on to the Methodist church.

With time to ourselves at last, in our quiet moments, between old folks' centres and drama groups and drives into the countryside, we often spoke of how far we had come since the day we made a stand to get on to the housing list. Perhaps the canvas-walled cubicle *did* get us on to the housing ladder … helped a little perhaps by my sit-in?

Notes from a schoolgirl's diary
By Sally Green

In this piece, Sally imagines a young girl's experience of VE Day.

THIS DIARY BELONGS TO: MARY HARRIS

AGE: 13 YEARS

YEAR: 1945

1945, a tumultuous year
All so often filled with fear

Tuesday 8 May 1945

Announced at 3.00 on the 8th of May
Victory in Europe, that glorious day!

This afternoon we sat in our kitchen all together, huddled around the table, the wireless on and none of us speaking. Mum, Grandad, Kathleen and I sat and waited. Even Jacko, our Jack Russell terrier, seemed to sense that something was up as he sat in his basket by the hearth, his little ears straight up as if standing to attention.

Soon enough, we heard on the wireless from London three loud bell strikes from Big Ben. It was three o'clock. Jacko sat up, startled and he was even trembling slightly. Through the crackling airwaves came Mr. Churchill's voice. He was talking, through the wireless, to us in our house and to all the people of Britain, wherever they were. His voice was deep and his words were serious. He sounded like Mr Turner, our Headmaster, in assembly when someone at school was in trouble for something.

Anyway, Mr Churchill said that all hostilities would end at one-minute past midnight tonight, Tuesday 8 May 1945.

None of us said anything, we just sat there and I felt very happy…

Wednesday 9 May 1945

There were people, people, everywhere
The bells rang out, the bonfires flared

Today, as well as yesterday, had been declared VE Day by Mr Churchill. So, this morning we were not quiet anymore; our house was filled with joy! We intended to make the most of this special day. Those sad feelings had gone and even

Mum was dancing round the kitchen which made Jacko bark and run around after her. Grandad just sat smiling in his armchair by the hearth; his face looked younger somehow. Kathleen and I ran straight down the stairs and out into the street to join our friends and neighbours and strangers too; it was as if we were one big family.

The bunting, the banners, the Union Jack flags
All lining the street to thank all 'our lads'

There was lots of noise everywhere! The brass band were playing up by the Town Hall, people were gathered in groups talking, some others were shouting, singing, larking about and some were even hugging each other too. Down the middle of the street was a long line of tables and people were bringing out what chairs they could find from their houses for a tea party. On the corner by the pub, old Frank Derbyshire was giving us some tunes on his trumpet and Danny Dixon had come to join him on his saxophone. So Kathleen and I went down to join them and dance around!

There was singing and dancing, the pubs they were crammed
Tea parties aplenty, all over the land

We all seemed so sad before, never knowing what might

happen each day. Today seemed like a dream and I never wanted it to end.

Kathleen and I teamed up with Billy from two doors up, Gwenny, his little sister, and Peggy Turner from across the road. We ran up and down the street lots of times, then we walked on the chairs all the way down until Uncle Bill caught us and told us to make ourselves useful and get the tea cups and saucers from Ma Davies at Number 38. Billy, Gwenny and I collected them and Peggy laid them all out, it took her ages. Then came the best bit when Mum, Auntie Jean and lots of people from the street started bringing out some food. We had fish and meat paste sandwiches, strawberries and jelly. It was the best tea party ever!

Civic Services were held and the Boys' Brigade marched
The trumpets they sounded, it touched all our hearts

At four o'clock there was to be a civic service of thanksgiving in the Town Hall. Grandpa had put on his best suit for it. Before we left for the service, he asked Kathleen and I to sit on the floor beside him as he sat in his chair by the hearth.

Destroyed families forever, privations and suffering
For them only tears, no noise or rejoicing

He said to us that while we, in Palmer Street, were very happy, we must also think of all the people that could not be happy on this day. There were many, many families that had lost loved ones in the fighting; what must it be like for them today, knowing their loved ones were not coming home? I shuddered thinking of them in their sad homes with empty places that could not be filled again. I wanted to cry.

Remember as well, those troops elsewhere
The Far East and Pacific, no victory was there

Grandad carried on and reminded us that while we were celebrating, in the Far East and Pacific the hostilities continued; many of our armed forces were still fighting, still being killed there as no resolution had yet been found. How awful to think that fighting was still happening! That gave me a big jolt and I thought how lucky our family had been.

Are we numb to the pain?
Of troops far away and so many slain?

Grandad said it was time to go, so Kathleen took one of his hands and I the other as we walked together to join the long line of people going into the Town Hall.

But they would not want sadness, they would not want fear
So, rejoice in the country that they held so dear
They fought for our freedom, huge parts did they play
In battle they struggled through those tortuous days
Their strength and their spirit were second to none
At last we could celebrate that this day had come

I wonder, if during my lifetime, I will ever record such an important day again.
Good-night, diary…

We shall always remember this V E Day
Our forces so courageous, so many, so brave.

The Evacuee
By Penny Harden

Penny writes: These are the recollections of a child who was evacuated during the war, as told to me. For some evacuees, the experience was a positive one: not so for this little boy. As you read this account – which is at times heart-rending – you might wonder how a parent could possibly bear to send a small child away for such a long period of time. The answer is simply that they believed that it was the best way of protecting their child from the bombs which were raining down on major cities, particularly London – and so they put their children into the hands of others, trusting that the child's well-being would be at the heart of this 'safe-guarding' system. These were not 'normal' times, and difficult decisions had to be made.

I recall only snapshots from my childhood evacuation from war-torn London, in 1940 – understandably, given that I was aged only two years and ten months. Fundamental changes to my life were about to unfold. Together, these sudden changes heightened my childhood insecurities about identity and about being loveable and loved. My separation from my mother was to last until 1944, when I was seven-plus, during which there were only occasional short visits from her and even fewer from my father. My father was in the army and spent much time in the Middle East. He was later discharged on medical grounds with stomach ulcers.

My first memory of being evacuated was of travelling by train from London, and looking out of a window at the countryside with its vast fields and hedgerows. My next memory was being in the passenger seat of a car in the main street of Bishop's Stortford. My brother, a year and ten months younger, lay swaddled on the back seat but with whom I can't remember. We were being taken to our destination, the country house and estate of Audley End, near Saffron Waldon in Essex, owned by Lord and Lady Braybrooke, but commandeered by the government for the duration of the war. Whilst the building itself was still occupied by its owners, they remained invisible from us, secluded behind closed doors along the corridors on the ground floor.

On arrival, I can recall quite clearly turning off the main road toward the huge impressive iron entrance gates, standing wide open on strong, tall stone columns, and the sweeping drive along which I was to be transported. Once inside, I remember the many other children all around: so many, but none that I knew. There were many 'nurse-type' adults into whose hands we were entrusted; they would care for us for however long it took for each of us to be relocated. But there was no particular 'mother figure' with whom I felt I could identify: no-one to make me feel special or loved. I can remember only snap-shots of events whilst here, like the enormous many-bedded dormitory nursery, which was rather stark and forbidding, lacking any sense of homeliness to a young child's eye.

I remember my first and only Christmas in this grand house, before I was moved on. My mother and father arrived with presents, mine being a little green wooden engine which my father had made for me, and for my young brother, a wooden tank. After the visitors had left, all the children played with their own toys in the dining room. I recall being jealous of my brother because, during play, a wheel fell off my little green engine, which upset me greatly, whilst my brother's tank remained intact.

Another memory was an occasion when all the children were taken out in a crocodile, two by two, for a walk in the grounds. We were each togged up in wellington boots and raincoats. There was some confusion as nurses tried to match the correct sized wellies to the right child, from what appeared to me to be a huge mountain of these boots.

And then there was this. I was waiting alone outside, when I was approached by a lady whose smile – directed at me – produced a warm thrill which suffused my entire body. I was not used to being the object of anyone's particular friendly intentions and I remember this isolated episode with such gratitude and, still at eighty years-plus, become emotional when I recall it: for it was the single time that I could recall anyone taking an interest in me.

This lady took me inside and sat me at a window-seat where I stayed dutifully for some time. I have a feeling that I was waiting for my parents and was clutching a miniature red post-box savings tin, which in my frustration I was banging hard against the window-sill, trying to destroy it. It must have been something that my parent had given me. My younger brother does not figure in this episode as far as I can remember.

In the next 'snapshot', I'm walking outside the house in the gardens – with whom, I'm unable to say. I see prisoners-of-war standing around with rakes and shovels. There is a brick wall, part of which has collapsed or broken through and somebody, way beyond the wall, is running, whilst a lot of shouting is going on.

And then there was another time. My parents had arrived (presumably to take me to some other place) and my father, mother and I had just come down the huge wooden staircase and were standing on a small landing looking over the bannister. On the floor below stood the lovely lady who had smiled at me. I believe my parents were in conversation with her. I was mesmerised, hoping against hope that this lady would acknowledge me – but she did not. The adults' conversation finished and this lady turned away, without a word or look in my direction, and disappeared through the doorway close by. I think that snub broke my heart. I have never forgotten it. It hurts to this very day.

Later, on the ground floor proper, we three came to another staircase under which quite a few bicycles were stacked. Lying underneath was my 'forgotten' little brother on his back, kicking and screaming, whilst my parents and several nurses were calling and pleading with him to come out. I'm assuming that my parents had come to take both of us away. While I was going without objection, my baby brother did not want to leave Audley End, where he had arrived as a baby and had been feted and pampered throughout our stay.

I did not feel like that at all about Audley End. But, when I look back and reflect on it, my period there was a far preferable experience to any of those which followed during the remaining, the longest period, of my wartime evacuation. I was a small child. I could only endure what was to come.

NB Following our evacuee relocations, Audley End was taken over by the SOE (Special Operations Executives), for use in training for operational espionage in France. The extensive grounds and gardens of the estate were maintained by Italian POW's throughout the period of the War. I can recall the POW gardeners quite clearly but no communication took place between us.

René Sethren
By Dianne Long

Dianne, the newest member of our group, came originally from South Africa. Her father had the highly unusual honour of having a ship named after him: here, she explains how this came about. (Ed)

It was 30th June 1941, and my father, René Sethren, was the chief petty officer aboard the HMSAS Southern Isles, a converted whaler. The ship's task was to perform anti-submarine patrols and give general support duties to the convoy. It was amongst a small flotilla of ships on convoy from Mersa Matruh approaching Tobruk – part of the Commonwealth forces, with the South Africans right at the centre , defending Tobruk and El Alamein.

As they closed in on the coast, their convoy came under fire from German shore batteries and was also attacked by a number of German Stuka dive bombers, JU87s and Messerschmidt 109s. First , five JU-88s attacked but without any real damage. This was followed by a lull and then the bigger and fiercer attack came. They were under attack from fifty enemy aircraft. The sky appeared to rain bombs.

René had been performing stoker duties for twelve

hours but as a qualified reserve machine gunner he was needed on deck. The body of his best friend was lying next to the twin Lewis anti-tank machine gun. Climbing onto ammunition boxes he started a nonstop volley of fire against the attacking German aircraft. The Stuka was joined by a JU88 and he was hit by machine gun bullets. He stood up and continued firing until the aircraft went down in flames.

The medics counted a total of twenty seven wounds to his legs, arm and side. The wounds were so extensive that he spent eighteen months recovering in hospital and would never be able to go to sea again. He was released on medical grounds on 19th June 1943.

René was awarded the CGM for conspicuous gallantry while serving in the Mediterranean Theatre 42nd Anti-Sub Group, and he attended the Victory Parade as one of the South African representatives. He received his gallantry decoration from King George VI. His medals are on display in the National Museum of Military History in Johannesburg, and as the most highly decorated South African in WW2, he and his family were asked to appear on a short film for Movietone at the cinema.

Later, in 1997, the SAS Oswald Pirow, a South African Navy fighting ship strike craft, was renamed the SAS RENÉ SETHREN in his honour, and this was sanctioned by Nelson Mandela.

My father never talked about the war and what happened to him, but my mother stored a pile of newspapers in her cupboard with cuttings about my dad's story. When we went to the beach we used to look at the massive scar travelling round his upper torso, where he had been shot during the war.

After the war, my father went to farm in the Transvaal on the ex-serviceman scheme. He was offered two oxen or fifteen donkeys as part of the deal, and decided on the donkeys. He grew maize and tomatoes.

It was here that I was born, in Groblersdal, near Middleburg. Life was quite hard. Mom looked after myself and my two sisters. There was a paraffin fridge on the verandah, and Dad used the battery from his car to work the old tractor. He had a motorbike with a sidecar attached to get around. He was very sociable and good-looking, the life and soul of any party. He had a great sense of humour, but there was also a darker side to him. I later found out that he had been bi-polar, which obviously affected his moods. He died when I was just seventeen years old: he would have celebrated his 100th birthday this year.

Billy Tomkins
By Jude Painter

*Jude's account of a fictional evacuee in the Mendips is based
on careful research from contemporary accounts; she is also
able to draw on her own background in farming. (Ed)*

I had not wanted to be evacuated, even though things were
bad in London and we never knew if our house would be
bombed or if we would be killed in the street. I had made a
promise to my father when he went off to fight: now I was
the man of the family I would take care of my mother and
Sonia, even Nan. But how could I do that if I was far away
in Somerset?

But in the end Mum made me go. She said that Sonia
should get away – she's a nervous child and I could see she
was becoming more jittery. Mum wanted her safe and calm
in the country and I couldn't let her go alone.

We were put with a family called Lee who had a farm
in the Mendip Hills not far from Cheddar. They were quite
kind to us, but I found it hard to get used to living in the
countryside. Most of our school was evacuated along with us
though, so many of my friends were staying nearby. We
found it hard to get along with the local children; they were

so different from us. The school was crowded, and the village kids seemed to hate us. There were playground fights every day and you could see that the teachers were finding it hard to cope.

Sonia settled better than I did at first, even though she felt a bit strange. She said that even the playground skipping games were different.The village girls asked lots of questions about what it was like in London and what new films they had watched before they were evacuated as films took ages to get to Cheddar. I think that the country girls found the evacuees interesting whereas the boys thought me and the other boys were a threat. To us they seemed like ignorant clodhoppers.

At first we found the country boring. There was nothing to do, people had to walk everywhere, we couldn't just hop on a bus or go to the pictures whenever we wanted. I took a while to get used to the cows. It surprised me how big they were, and I didn't like the way they followed us about and stared, as if they wanted something or were going to attack.

Sonia was still wetting the bed nearly every night as she had in London, even though she was eight. Mrs. Lee made sure she took her out to the privy in the garden before she went to bed and of course she had a pot under the bed which she could have used in the night. I was embarrassed for her, but Mrs Lee said it was just because of the shock of all the bombing and that she would get over it in time, probably.

At night if you went outside there were strange noises – foxes making odd sounds and owls screeching, even hedgehogs snuffling about. It was not at all quiet and we just never knew what was out there.

We noticed straight away that the food in the country, though, was much better, and we could have an egg everyday if we fancied one. There were little bantams' eggs as well as hens' eggs. The farmers didn't have a bacon ration if they didn't want one, instead they could keep, kill and salt one or two pigs a year for themselves. I thought about Mum and Nan and wished I could send some of our good food to them.

One day at school we had someone in from the Observer Corps come to talk to us about identifying planes. We London boys were red hot at this because we had seen so many and we knew all about different sorts of bombs and all had collections of shrapnel we had picked up from the streets. We showed that we knew a lot more than the country boys. The man spoke to us about writing down what the planes were and which direction they were flying in, so we could pass the message on. He told us that children could do a lot to help Britain, not just the picking berries and fruit for jam and gardening which we were already doing.

After the talk we drew planes which I was already good at. The local boys liked the drawings a lot and some of them asked me to teach them. Then things got better, and I didn't have so many fights. After I showed Paul Lee how to draw good planes, he seemed to become more friendly to me and showed me how to make a catapult and since then we go off playing together all the time.

Paul Lee's father is attached to the home guard and after he has finished milking and his farm work he goes to the village hall to do stuff about defence. He has a gun hanging on a beam in the kitchen and a pistol hidden in a drawer which Paul showed me. Mr. Lee is a very good shot because farmers are used to shooting rabbits for the pot, but even so, they still practice shooting every week and throwing grenades.

Paul and I wondered where his father went some days when he went off, so we followed him, without him knowing. We found out that he went to a cave near Rackley called Denny's Hole and wondered what on earth he could be doing there. Then we did some more investigation and found out that he and other local men are using this cave (and probably other ones) as secret hideouts where they store ammunition and supplies, even tinned food in case the Germans invade, this is something which nobody ever talks about.

One day when Mr. Lee was in a good mood he explained that if Hitler invaded England he would probably come in from the beaches. So now there are lots of bunkers and observation posts where people keep watch along on the coast all the time.

Now Paul has shown me how to cope with cows and told me to carry a stick. He says the only time I should worry about cows is if they have calves with them. All the farm animals in Britain are counted and written down by the Ministry of Agriculture so they can make sure there is enough food to go around and they do the same with the crops that farmers grow.

Now I have got to know the area better, I've found out that there are lots of secrets everywhere. People are storing supplies and soldiers are doing mysterious things in the hills and people transport things at night-time in covered carts. It is frightening if you stop to think about it, but exciting too.

Paul says the church bells all across the country will ring out if we are invaded and some of the men will go off and hide. Then they will come out and plant bombs and blow up bridges and roads to stop the Germans. People have already taken down a lot of the signposts and they've stopped selling maps in the shops to make to make it harder for strangers to find their way about.

All of us evacuees still worry about our families being bombed in towns and the fathers in the forces being killed, but people all over the country are working hard for the war effort which takes our minds off the worries a bit. Because Hitler did not invade in 1939 as they had first expected, we have had a bit more time to prepare ourselves in case he does come and the sea around Britain also helps to protect us. People probably pray more than they used to – I know I do.

References

Much of the information used in this fictional account has come from Somerset v Hitler, Secret Operations in the Mendips 1939-1945, *by Donald Brown.*

I have also referred to the excellent BBC online archive Britain at War.

Coming home
By Sue Purkiss

My father was a prisoner of war in what is now Poland for five years. He was captured on the way to Dunkirk in May 1940. For a long time he didn't speak about his experiences, and when he eventually did, it was mostly to tell us about funny things that happened, like the time the prisoners made hooch out of rotten potatoes and got the guards drunk on it.

For some time now I have been working on a novel which is loosely based on his experiences. This section is from near the end, when he was liberated from Fallingbostel Camp in western Germany, having been marched across Europe ahead of the advancing Russians.

They woke one morning to find that the German officers had melted away in the night, leaving behind only the few unfortunate guards who had nowhere else to go. RSM Lord swiftly took over, posting guards on the perimeter. Harry was with a man called Albert Taplow, who'd been captured just a few months before and so still had a uniform that was more-or-less correct. A German guard was with them too; he was all right, quite decent really. They were passing round a cigarette concocted from some vile mixture, and Taplow was regaling them with stories about RSM Lord – they'd been in the same unit and he had some tales to tell about the redoubtable sergeant major.

Then, above the laughter, they heard a distant rumble. The ground beneath their feet began to vibrate. They glanced at each other nervously.

Harry dropped the cigarette and ground it out with his foot. They stood up straighter and waited, tense and silent. The rumble grew louder till the sound almost deafened them, and then a massive tank rumbled round the bend in the road.

"What the hell's that?" said Harry, startled. He'd never seen such a vehicle, and he didn't recognise the white star painted on its side.

But a huge grin broke out on Taplow's face. "It's our boys!" he yelled. "That's their badge! It's the allies – they're here!"

The tank rolled to a stop. Harry couldn't get over the size of it: the tanks he'd seen in France had been puny compared to this. The lid of the turret flipped open and the tank commander appeared. He regarded the three men laconically, chewing gum. The eyes under the steel helmet were singularly unimpressed. He held a gun, and it was trained, quite casually, on the three of them.

"Don't shoot!" gabbled Taplow. "We're on your side!"

"*You* might be," drawled the man, "but what about these two jokers?"

Albert gestured towards Harry. "He's English, sir! He's just…"

Understanding, Harry glanced down at his precious Russian greatcoat. "I've been a prisoner since Dunkirk. The uniform fell apart after a bit," said Harry. He felt suddenly tired: he was sick of apologising, sick of explaining and making excuses. Suddenly his head was full of the experiences of the last five years – starvation and fear, wide rivers and huge forests, refugees and lost souls. Before him was this American with the easy confidence of the conqueror: behind him was the battered, crumbling edifice that was Europe. Harry was twenty four, but he felt as if he was about a hundred..

The American's attention shifted to the German.

"What about this one? He's German, ain't he? How's he treated you? Just say the word, and I'll…"

"No!" said Harry quickly. "Don't shoot him. He's all right. Leave him be."

The American shrugged. "Okay then, if you say so. Stand back, fellas. We're coming through."

And the tank drove straight through the fence, leaving the barbed wire scrawled untidily across the ground.

After that it was all very quick. Those who had been prisoners longest were taken first: driven to an Allied camp, showered, de-loused, issued with sparkling new uniforms, then taken to an airfield where they were loaded into Dakotas, thirty at a time, and flown back to England.

And that was it. For them, at last, the war really was over.

Some weeks later, after a spell in hospital to sort out some of the damage that near-starvation, not to mention Fleischer's boots, had done to his insides, Harry was issued with a ticket to Nottingham. He crossed the city to reach the bus station and was mildly surprised to find that there were still buses running; he'd thought he might have to walk the eight miles to Ilkeston. He felt a little bewildered as he gazed from the window of the bus: how was it that so little had changed here? He'd expected bomb damage – London had been almost flattened – but here there was almost none. He got off at Nottingham Road and walked up Cavendish Road, past the school, past rows of houses. Then he halted, confused. There was some sort of party going on outside his house – tables, bunting, banners. He didn't want to interrupt anything. He looked round uncertainly. A man was leaning against a gate, smoking.

"What's going on here?" said Harry, jerking his

thumb towards the festivities.

"Oh, it's all in aid of some bloke who's coming home from the war," said the man. "Been a prisoner for five years. Bit of a hero, so they say."

"Really?" said Harry faintly.

Then he saw a small woman coming out of his house. Her grey hair was pinned up in a bun, and her dark eyes met his and widened in astonishment. He began to walk towards her. Then he started to run.

After five long years, he was home.

That night, as he bent down to kiss his mother goodnight, she reached out, put her hands on his shoulders, and gazed at him searchingly.

"Harry," she said. "What was it really like? Was it *very* bad?"

He thought for a moment. Where to start? What to tell her? How *much* to tell her? But he already knew it wasn't possible. He couldn't put it into words, didn't even want to.

And so he began the long lie. "No," he said, with a little smile that tried, unsuccessfully, to draw attention away from the bleakness in his eyes. "It wasn't too bad at all, not really."

As he turned away to climb the stairs, he sneezed, and he realised he had the beginnings of a sore throat. And it struck him that in all those long five years of hunger and deprivation, he hadn't caught a single cold. Not one.

Liberated British POWs at Fallingbostel

Memories of the war in Somerset
By Heather Redman

This is not the first time Heather has written about what happened when, as a child, she met a German prisoner of war who came to work near the cottage where she and her family lived. Her story became the inspiration for a book produced in Wells by a children's book group. It was called Heather's Bracelet, *and caused quite a sensation, with Heather being interviewed on television and even being kissed on the cheek by Michael Morpurgo! There is a colour picture of her bracelet on the back cover of this book. (Ed)*

Being just a baby when the war started, I wasn't aware of all the preparations – the Anderson shelters that were built in people's gardens, for instance, and the search light bases on hills and in places where the German planes could be brought down without doing too much damage to buildings and people on the ground.

It didn't take long for all the men to be called up, and then the women took over the men's jobs and got busy making bombs. Not a job for a lady in the thirties – but this was a war to change the world. The first thing my mother did was to move house. She moved us from a farm cottage to a house about a mile away. There was a searchlight across the next field. This made it dangerous, but no-one could tell her different – she knew best.

In December 1940 our war took a turn for the worse. Mother received a letter to say my father was missing. As well as this, I was involved in an accident with a car and my brother was in bed with chicken pox. But we all survived. My father was found in hospital in Ireland and invalided out of the army with a weak heart, and I was sent home from hospital with no bones broken but covered in chicken pox spots. We carried on, hoping the war would soon be over.

Father found us a new house, or at least a couple of rooms tacked on to his uncle's house – which meant that there was no rent to pay so he had more money to spend in the pub. Mother was overjoyed to get away from our nasty neighbours and quite happy to look after Uncle George and his nephew. So now she had two houses to clean, two wash days and two sets of meals to get ready twice a day. We had no electricity and no water in the house, so Mother would take our washing into the shed where our tap and boiler were kept. I never heard her grumble once.

I grumbled all the time. The doctor told her not to let me cry, because since the accident I used to hold my breath and turn blue, but I always made a fuss when the weekly bath time came round. She would take the tin bath down from the wall in the shed, put two kettles of boiling water in it, then cool it down. I had about five minutes before I was hounded out so my brother could have his bath before the water cooled down. Then I had to be carried into the house and put on the settle in front of the fire wrapped in a small thin towel. Summer was all right, but quite a few baths were missed in the winter.

The planes were still going across the sky dropping their bombs, and so we would get up in the night till the all-clear siren sent us back to bed and hopefully to sleep. One night a bomb came down in the apple tree outside our window, but we didn't know it had happened till years later as it didn't explode. These were my school years, hateful times for someone like me who didn't like doing as I was told.

It was when I was seven that the war became real to me. I came home from school and walking down the lane I was overtaken by a big army lorry which stopped outside our house.

A soldier carrying a gun jumped out of the lorry and went round the back and opened it up. A crowd of Italian prisoners of war jumped out with rakes and shovels and started cleaning the ditches. One prisoner was left to make a fire and cook a meal, and the driver of the lorry, who was a German officer, sat in the lorry making pretty bracelets which the Italians sold for him. On closer inspection he was, with his shiny golden hair and piercing blue eyes, the most beautiful man I had ever seen – I was in love!.

Now as I came home from school I was drawn to the lorry and the handsome officer. First it was just smiles; a couple of days later I said hello; and then I began to stop and talk to him, kidding myself I was teaching him English.

Sometimes I just sat on the wheel arch of the lorry watching him making his bracelets. With just a strip of a cocoa tin and some plastic string, a small knife and his fingers, he could make a beautiful piece of jewellery.

Then one day my father came home early and ordered me indoors. He said the German was the enemy, and I must keep away from the lorry. But my mother was on my side.

"He's some mother's son, and I don't expect he wants to be in a war any more than you or I. Leave the girl alone!"

Next day I was back on the lorry. One day he asked me what my favourite colour was. A couple of days later he gave me a beautiful red bracelet. My mother told me to give it back because we couldn't afford it, but he insisted that it was a present and I could keep it – I still have it.

A couple of days later the lorry didn't turn up – they'd moved to a new place. I never saw my soldier again. Not too much time later the war ended. One day we went to see the house I was born in. It was an empty shell, with the front garden buried under a heap of rubble.

Mother always knew best.

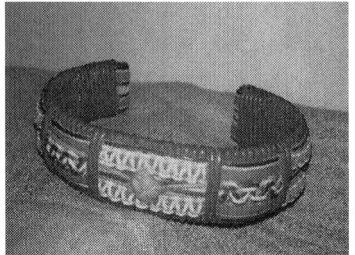

The Women's Land Army 1917-1919 and 1939-1949
By Caroline Woolley

Had I been born some 20 years earlier I know I would have been a member of the Women's Land Army, whose members, despite much prejudice, did so much to keep the home fires burning during two world Wars. Instead I was introduced to agriculture in the late 1950s when I cycled about five miles from home in north Bristol to a farm in south Gloucestershire. At that point I had never laid hand to a cow and was only vaguely aware of the business end. A few years later I attended what was then called Somerset Farm Institute at Cannington to learn more about the industry.

Throughout my adult life I have maintained a link with farming and the college where I studied. During the 1980s I found myself becoming very interested in the lives of those who had gone before me. At the Farm Institute – by this time known as Somerset College of Agriculture and Horticulture – an annual magazine was produced by an active Old Students' Association. I became a member and eventually was appointed editor.

As the college changed focus and was taken over by Bridgwater Further Education College to become a mere department, it became abundantly obvious that as a stand-

alone entity, the old Somerset Farm Institute of my formative years had disappeared. In response to this, A Chronicle of Cannington, an A4 paperback with over 200 pages, was published in 2006 by what was left of the Old Student Association. It provided a collection of facts, photographs of decades of students, and anecdotal stories.

Sadly, very few stories appeared chronicling the experiences of the thousands of girls who tilled, milked and sheared sheep throughout those war years, many of whom attended training courses at the old SFI. But Edna Liddell from West Somerset, sadly no longer with us, did provide an account, and this is included in the following article.

Toward the end of the 1930s, as war became increasingly likely, the government wanted to increase the amount of food grown within Britain. To do this, more help was needed on the farms and so the government started the second Women's Land Army in June 1939, based on an earlier First World War scheme. By1944 it had over 80,000 members and it lasted until official disbandment on 21 October 1949.

This was a mobile agricultural labour force of women who were specially recruited to assist in increasing the production of home-grown food during both World Wars, as men were called up to join the fighting forces. Its role was particularly important because imported food supplies were being destroyed through enemy action at sea, which successive governments feared might result in the starvation of the nation.

The WLA had been first instituted in Great Britain in 1917, some three years into the First World War, when it was reported that the food supplies of this country were seriously menaced both immediately and in the future. It was seen as imperative that a strong and suitable women's work force should come forward to work on the land.

As in 1917, the purpose of the 1939 version was to recruit, equip and supply girls and women from non-agricultural occupations between the ages of 18 and 40 for regular full-time employment in agriculture, to supplement the ordinary sources of agricultural labour during the period of the emergency.

Of course there was a general reluctance throughout the agricultural community around employing women directly into farm work. The WLA had to overcome prejudice as well as new and difficult working conditions if it was to be successful. The practical aspects certainly challenged the status quo among the nations' farmers. There was the formulation of national policies at government level to set up the WLA to take into account; the recruitment of its membership; policies on the accommodation and welfare of recruits; and the training, work and conditions of service which would all be needed to form a country wide network.

Woman at work!

Daughters of landowners joined the WLA and participated in the making of national policy in a period when male decision makers dominated rural and urban contexts. While WLA recruits performed practical agricultural tasks, many of which were consistent with traditional views on what was appropriate work for women – for example horticulture and the care of livestock – the status quo continued to be challenged. Tasks such as fieldwork, tractor driving and the operation of mechanical implements formerly considered to be beyond the physical and mental capacities of women were performed with gusto!

For many years the contribution of the WLA to British agriculture was overlooked by the industry in general. However in 2002 Margaret Bullock wrote a doctoral thesis centred on the Land Army in a small area of the former West Yorkshire; it was published through the School of Education of Leeds University.

Her work is referred to in this overview.

Many of the young women never went back to their urban roots. Some found themselves husbands. Others just enjoyed the work and preferred country life to town life. But these 'lucky ones', who stayed often took on a much harder life than they could have imagined, because life on the farm year in year out was not for the faint hearted in those austere times.

In the West Country, the majority of farms are run by families, so this meant that the young women were dispatched at random to family farms. Most of the girls lived on the farms where they worked but, in many rural situations, the living conditions could be very basic, and the way of life lonely; and as a result, many girls felt vulnerable. Some placements were very tricky indeed. Hostels for the girls to live in were set up and by 1944, 22,000 of the land girls were living in about 700 hostels.

So, who exactly were these young women? From where were they recruited?

Posters were placed throughout the country, mostly in towns and cities, encouraging young women to 'do their bit' for the war effort. Many were lured by the healthy fresh air of the countryside and the desire to help, and they applied in droves.

The majority of the land girls already lived in the countryside, but more than a third came from London and the industrial cities of the north of England. A separate branch was set up in 1942 for forestry industry work, officially known as the

Women's Timber Corps. Its members were colloquially known as "Lumber Jills". This was disbanded in 1946.

There were quite a lot of rules for the girls to follow. For example, there was a uniform that had to be worn when working. Paperwork was created for the replacement of missing kit and strictly adhered to. The uniform provided was as follows.

Hat – cowboy style
Shirts – 3
Green tie - 1
Pullover – 2 green
Breeches – 2 prs brown, either twill or corduroy
Dungarees 2 prs
Overall coats – 2
Long Socks – 6 pairs long woolen
Brown overalls – 1 pr
WLA arm band
Slipper socks (if gumboots issued) 1 pr
Shoes or boots either or depending on occupation
Gumboots or substitute boots and leggings
Oilskin or mackintosh

Following a period of training suitable for the tasks to be done and suitably clad, the girls sallied forth into the mysteries of agriculture. About 25% of them were involved in milking cows, mostly by hand. Conditions would have been very rough on delicate hands not used to practical work but nonetheless many girls who had never experienced the countryside turned up for work in full 'killer' make-up – well, as much as possible given the restrictions at the time. But they soon realized that this was a pointless exercise for daytime and kept their precious make up for social occasions – were they lucky enough to have a social life. Remember, agriculture is a solitary occupation.

One of the less pleasant aspects of the countryside is rats. These posed a serious problem and threat to supplies of food and animal fodder. Teams of land girls were trained to work in anti-vermin squads. They were also trained to dispose of foxes, rabbits and moles

The farming work included clearing land; stone picking; weeding; thistle cutting; manure spreading; singling and hoeing turnips; potato setting and lifting; vegetable planting and transplanting; milking; stock tending and rearing; butter and cheese making; poultry rearing; hay making; harvesting; sheep shearing; thatching; stacking corn; ploughing; loading and unloading sacks of corn; threshing; fruit and hop picking; reed stripping; bark peeling; timber felling; gardening and varied horticultural duties.

A Land Girl at work

Conscription was introduced in Dec 1941 as an alternative to one of the auxiliary services for women – the WACS, the Wrens or the WAAF. The girls were paid less than men – twenty eight shillings per week (£3.36) for a 48 hour winter week or a 50 hour summer week. Men were paid thirty eight shillings per week (£4.56), no holidays, but a free travel pass every 6 months. Changes were implemented as time went by.

Following the disbanding of the WLA in 1950, relatively little attention was paid to the achievements of the agricultural women in comparison to those in munitions or manufacturing, in either academic study or in the popular media. However, with celebrations to mark the Jubilee events of 2002 the WLA made a re-appearance, both nationally and locally. This included accounts of former recruits meeting up 50 years after they first met in the WLA and a series of photographs showing the WLA at work on the land in the 1940s.

An extensive booklet entitled *Women at War* which includes short articles on individuals serving in the auxiliary services including the WLA was published in early 2001.

A film entitled *The Land Girls* was released in 1998 based on a book of the same name. It gave a somewhat romantic view. But one reviewer considered the film to be a "moving tribute to a sometimes forgotten band of heroines who, quite literally, kept the home fires burning with their hard slog and toil."

And it should never be forgotten that without the decision to introduce the specially recruited mobile labour force of women to agricultural work and their toil over a period of 11 years, the production of the nation's food supplies in a period of great hardship would have been greatly reduced, possibly with disastrous results.

Should you wish to investigate further the contribution to the War Effort made by these women, please go to your computer and look up *The Women's Land Army 1939 – 1950*, by Dr. Margaret Bullock.

Unfortunately there is little personal documentation

available and as 2020 is long way from 1940, there are only a handful of WLA ladies still with us. However, one account of the WLA experienced by Edna Liddle of Somerset appeared in an Old Student magazine of Somerset Farm Institute. As a past student 1961 – 62, I had access to all of these magazines, many of which were edited and published in *A Chronicle of Cannington* in 2006. Here are Edna's unabridged words.

The Women's Land Army – Edna Liddle

In 1940 my job finished – owing to the war we all had to help in war work. I was sent to a munitions factory, which did not suit me, neither did taking bus fares as a bus conductress. So I became a Land Army girl. I had no experience of the work but I knew I wanted to be in the open air.

I put my bicycle, suitcase and myself on the train at Paddington and later that day arrived at Wiveliscombe station. The farmer met me with his horse and a very dirty putt (cart) and, in due course, we arrived at Tolland. The farmhouse was small and I had no luxury of a bedroom but slept at the top of the stairs for the next 3 and a half years. Water for washing had to be fetched from the stream and all drinking water was drawn from a well some 200 yards from the house.

I soon found out that being a Land Girl was far removed from being a certified flower maker and shop assistant at Marshall and Snelgrove of Oxford Street. Land Army girls were expected to do a man's work. Hedging, ditching and shearing were some of the jobs and if the farmer could make a fool of you he often would and get a good laugh out of it.

The most painful was learning to help milk 30 – 40 cows by hand and this played havoc with the sinews and tendons of my hands and arms. My first job was daunting. I was shown a ten acre field covered with heaps of dung, given a fork and told to get on with spreading – this to be done in my new white Land Army mac.

I got on well working with horses – we spent many hours 'dragging', harrowing, ploughing and hauling. The animals seemed to know I was 'green' and I'm sure they helped me. As time went on I found the work easier and my love of the countryside increased. Whilst cutting kale one morning a hunted fox came right up beside me and hid from the hounds.

I enjoyed cutting 'binds' but when we were threshing Barley it could be quite uncomfortable with the pieces sticking everywhere. Haymaking and harvesting were such hard work as all the moving of hay and straw was done by hand. Just for a moment consider the labour involved in haymaking in the 1940s. Two horses pulling a mowing machine, hay left for two days, then turned with horse drawn *machinery. When dry, two rows turned into one then loaded manually onto a wagon, unloaded and put either into barn or rick (the latter having to be thatched). Feeding the hay meant cutting out slabs with a hay knife and carting to the stock – a far cry from today's methods.*

After nine years I received a long service badge but I loved farm life so much that I continued for another ten. During these years I attended Cannington (Somerset) Farm Institute and successfully completed courses in Dairy Work and Milking and my first savings were accumulated when a farmer gave me one bull and one heifer calf instead of overtime money and they bred many Shorthorn calves.

My Land Army years were happy ones and in 1950 I marred a fellow farm worker but continued farming until I became a Mum. The war certainly altered the course of many lives but in my experience it was for the better – a good way of life.

A statue commemorating the Women's Land Army girls has been placed in the National Arboretum, not far from Tetbury in Gloucestershire.

.

Printed in Poland
by Amazon Fulfillment
Poland Sp. z o.o., Wrocław

57955340R00047